Graphic Novels
Available from Papercutz

1 Scars!
2 Drownings!
3 Vultures!
$7.95 each in paperback
$12.95 each in hardcover

ZORRO ®

#3 "VULTURES!"

DON McGREGOR • Writer
SIDNEY LIMA • Artist
Based on the character created by
JOHNSTON McCULLEY

New York

This is for my Grandson, KRISTOFFER MOURITZEN, who at 2 years old already knows what he likes and doesn't like — is already a force of independent nature in his own right —and is an expressive story-teller, who uses his voice and face and hands to bring the story home, stories that would make some people's jaws drop if we did them in comics. –D.M.

Vultures!
DON McGREGOR — Writer
SIDNEY LIMA — Artist
MARK LERER — Letterer
MARCOS De MIRANDA — Colorist
JIM SALICRUP — Editor-In-Chief

ISBN 10: 1-59707-020-3 paperback edition
ISBN 13: 978-1-59707-020-1 paperback edition
ISBN 10: 1-59707-021-1 hardcover edition
ISBN 13: 978-1-59707-021-8 hardcover edition

10   9   8   7   6   5   4   3   2   1

WE NEED TO RIDE UP THE CANYON-SIDE, EULALIA.

OKAY, IF YOU SAY SO, DON DI... ZORRO.

AS WE PASS THROUGH HERE, I AM OVERWHELMED NOT JUST BY THE BEAUTY...THE GRANDEUR...OR THE SHEER DIVERSITY OF THIS PLACE.

I AM OVERCOME WITH A FEELING THAT I AM IN A PLACE THAT SPEAKS TO THE DAWN OF TIME.

IN JAIL, THE J-MAN DIDN'T HAVE TO GO RIDING DOWN SOME STEEP MOUNTAIN SLOPE. LIKELY GET MYSELF KILLED DOING IT!

AND, ON TOP OF THAT, IN JAIL, YOU DIDN'T HAVE TO SOCIALIZE, IF YOU DIDN'T WANT.

YOU DIDN'T HAVE TO TRY TO ACT LIKE EVERYBODY ELSE. OTHER PRISONERS, THEY DON'T MUCH EXPECT YOU TO BE NORMAL. BEEN MY EXPERIENCE, THE REAL TWISTED ONES ARE THE PEOPLE WHO BELIEVE THEY KNOW WHAT NORMAL IS.

OF COURSE, PRISONERS ARE LIKE EVERYBODY ELSE, THEY HAVE TO LABEL YOU. I DIDN'T MUCH LIKE BEING LABELED THE J-MAN AT FIRST, BUT TRUTH TO TELL, I'VE GROWN TO LIKE IT.

I AM THE JAIL-MAN, OUT OF HIS ELEMENT IN THE WIDE OPEN SPACES, BUT WHAT ARE YOU GOING TO DO?

OUT HERE, WHEN YOU'RE IN THE MIDDLE OF NOWHERE, ONE THING IS, NOT MANY PEOPLE ARE GOING TO TELL YOU YOU'RE NUTS FOR TALKING TO YOURSELF.

I'D TELL ANY-BODY ANYHOW, THE BEST CONVERSATIONS THE J-MAN EVER HAD WAS WITH HIMSELF!

PHWEET!

DID YOU SAY, "JAILMAN"?

YEAH. A TOTAL NUTCASE. I THINK HE KNOWS LOCKSPUR HAS TAKEN OVER AND HE RESENTS IT.

I'VE HEARD HIM TALKING TO HIMSELF ABOUT WHAT A COLD HEART HE THINKS LOCKSPUR HAS. THINKS LOCKSPUR'S TRYING TO CHEAT HIM OUT OF EVERYTHING. FOR ALL I KNOW, THE J-MAN COULD BE RIGHT.

YET, IN THE END, I THINK HE KNOWS LOCKSPUR HAS THE FORCE OF PERSONALITY TO CALL THE SHOTS. LITERALLY. AND HE GETS THE J-MAN TO OVERSEE THE DIRTY WORK.

LOCKSPUR'S GOING TO KILL HER.

HER?

THE WIDOW CANIFF. NORMANDIE CANIFF. A WONDERFUL WOMAN. HER HUSBAND, PATRICK, JUST DIED. PATRICK WAS ONE OF THE LEADING ILLUSTRATORS OF OUR TIME.

"LOCKSPUR BILLS HIMSELF AS A PLAINSMAN. A GUIDE TO UNKNOWN PLACES.

"HE BEFRIENDS THEM, YOU SEE. THE HUSBAND AND WIFE. IN THEIR LATER YEARS.

"HE PROMISES THEM ADVENTURES AS THEY HAVE NEVER SEEN IN THEIR LIFE. HE INSINUATES HIMSELF INTO THE COUPLE'S LIVES."

BUT AFTER WHAT I OVERHEARD HIM SAYING TO THE J-MAN, I CAME TO REALIZE THIS WASN'T JUST AN ADVENTURE HE WAS BRINGING INTO THEIR LIVES. HE WAS GETTING EVERYTHING THEY HAD. AND THIS TREK WOULD COST THEM MORE THAN MONEY. LOCKSPUR WOULD SEE TO IT THAT THIS WAS THEIR LAST EXPLORATION...OF ANY KIND!

THAT'S SOME BITE YOU HAVE, TORNADO. I NEVER REALIZED.

I DIDN'T REALIZE MY HEART COULD... BEAT SO HARD... IT FEELS LIKE IT MIGHT... BURST...OUT OF MY CHEST!

NOT...THAT I DOUBTED...FOR A SECOND...THAT YOU'D COME THROUGH!

SO, THIS LOCKSPUR'S CONTINUING ON HIS WAY TO THIS LETHAL DESTINATION. ONCE THERE, HE WILL KILL THE SENORA.

AS A MAN WHO LOVES WOMEN AND ART, I CANNOT LET THIS HAPPEN.

BEFORE THEY SPOTTED ME, I HEARD LOCKSPUR SAY HE WOULD CLAIM NORMANDIE DIED IN A MISADVENTURE. HER BODY WOULD BE LOST IN THE BUBBLING, BOILING MUD CAULDRON.

SO SAD, HE'LL REPORT ON HIS RETURN TO HER HOME, SO SEEMINGLY SINCERE. HE'LL HAVE THAT WRITTEN DOCUMENT SIGNED BY HER IN HAND, GIVING HIM ACCESS TO THE ESTATE.

TO THE ART.

WHICH HE'LL POSSESS.

EITHER JUST TO OWN IT...TO HOARD IT...AND MAYBE SELL SOME TO GAIN A LUXURIOUS LIFE-STYLE.

EULALIA, I NEED YOU TO STAY WITH SENOR GOULD WHILE I TRACK THIS J-MAN.

I'M SURE HE WILL LEAD ME TO THE CARAVAN.

WHY ME? YOU THINK HE NEEDS A WOMAN'S TOUCH, WHATEVER THAT'S SUPPOSED TO MEAN? I DON'T KNOW ANYTHING ABOUT HEALING WOUNDS.

I KNOW A FEW THINGS ABOUT AMOROUS ENDEAVORS. I'D DARE SAY, I KNOW AS MUCH AS THE FOX.

BUT I ADMIT MY LIMITS. THE FOX KNOWS MORE ABOUT MEDICINE THAN I DO.

AND WHAT LITTLE I KNOW I LEARNED FROM BERNARDO.

AH, YESSS! YOUR DEAR FRIEND AND AIDE, THE ONE EVERYONE THINKS IS DEAF AND MUTE, BACK IN YOUR REAL LIFE, OR HOWEVER YOU THINK OF LIFE BACK IN LOS ANGELES AND AT THE DE LA VEGA HACIENDA.

I DON'T HAVE TIME TO DEBATE THIS WITH YOU, EULALIA. A WOMAN'S LIFE IS AT STAKE.

A WOMAN'S LIFE IS ALWAYS AT STAKE!

SUPPOSING THE BAD GUYS KILL YOU AND YOU NEVER GET BACK TO ME? WHAT HAPPENS THEN?

SOMEHOW, EULALIA, WITH YOUR SKILLS AND WILL POWER AND INGENUITY, I HAVE NO DOUBT YOU WILL SURVIVE AND THRIVE. AND PERHAPS SCARCELY MISS ME.

BUT THE FOX HAS NO PLANS TO DIE! SO DON'T WRITE ME OFF SO QUICKLY.

STAY HERE, AND I'LL BE BACK WITHIN A DAY OR TWO.

STAY, MY EYE!

COME ON, SENOR GOULD. YOU WANTED AN ADVENTURE. YOU'VE GOT ONE.

IF HE CAN FOLLOW YOUR VILLAIN, I'LL HAVE NO PROBLEM FOLLOWING HIM.

I'VE MADE A CARRY-A-BODY FROM BRANCHES AND SUCH BEFORE. YOU DO IT ONCE, YOU CAN DO IT AGAIN. RIGHT, SENOR GOULD?

WHATEVER YOU SAY, YOU-LARL-EEE-A. DID I SAY THAT RIGHT?

CLOSE ENOUGH.

I LIKE PRETTY PICTURES.

I'M SURE YOU DO. AS LONG AS THERE AREN'T ANY COMPLICATED WORDS TO GO ALONG WITH THE PRETTY PICTURES AND MESS THEM UP, RIGHT, J-MAN?

HOW'D YOU KNOW THAT?

JUST A GUESS.

ANYHOW, WE'LL CAMP TONIGHT AT THE MUD VOLCANO, AND I'LL GET HER TO PUT HER JOHN HANCOCK TO DOCUMENT, AND THEN I'LL KILL HER.

YOU MEAN YOU'LL HAVE ME KILL HER.

WHATEVER.

RRRUSSHHHHHHRRRROOAARRRRRRRRUSSHHHHRRRUSSHHHH

I SEE YOU DIDN'T TAKE OFF MY MASK.

WHY WOULD THE J-MAN CARE WHO YOU ARE? JUST BE ANOTHER FACE I WOULDN'T RECOGNIZE MOST LIKELY.

AND EVEN IF I DID, IT WOULDN'T MEAN MUCH MORE TO ME. WHAT THE J-MAN CARES ABOUT IS, MASKED, UNMASKED, YOU CAN'T INTERFERE WITH LOCKSPUR'S PLANS FOR THE SNOOTY WIDOW.

AND THE J-MAN PAYS YOU BACK FOR KILLING HIS PRIZED, ADORED TWIN MUSKET.

RR...UURRRR...SPLURTT...RRUURRRRRSH

SPLURTT...SPLURTT...SPLURTT.RRRRUURRRR...RRRUUUUR

MAY THE SAINTS SAVE ME FROM OBSESSED COLLECTORS!

WHUSK

SPLURTT...SPLURTT...SPLURTT...RRRRUURRRR...SPLUSHSHSS

WE WIN!

RRRUUUUR...SPLURTT...SPLURTT...SPLURTT...RRRRUUURRR

WE GET EVERYTHING WE WANT!

YOU? YOU'RE JUST A LOSER WHO LOSES EVERYTHING!

NO VULTURES FEEDING HERE. YOU KNOW. THE TREES SEEM TO MOCK US, REMINDING US THEY LIVED LONG BEFORE WE LIVED. AND WILL BE HERE LONG AFTER WE'RE GONE.

LOCKSPUR DID NOT LIE ABOUT THE UNIQUE QUALITIES OF THIS PLACE WHEN HE DESCRIBED IT TO NORMANDIE, AND CONVINCED HER TO TRAVEL OUT HERE.

WHICH DOESN'T MEAN LOCKSPUR, OR HIS CRAZED PARTNER, THAT J-MAN, WON'T KILL.

I'D LIKE THE FOX NOT TO GET HIMSELF DEAD.

AND KEEP HIS PROMISE TO FIND ME A NEW LIFE.

THE SMELL GOES DEEP INTO MY HEAD EVERY TIME I BREATHE. WHAT MAKES IT SO MALODOROUS?

SULFUR, MAYBE. YES, I BELIEVE THAT IS WHAT IT IS.

WE HEAR AND SMELL THE MUD VOLCANO'S HEART, WHICH IS AT THE CENTER OF THE WORLD.

RRUUU...RRSPLUSHSPLURTT...RRRUUUURSS

"WE SPEAK OF ITS HEART LIKE THE HEART YOUR HUSBAND PUTS INTO HIS ART.

SPLURTT...RRRUUUUR...SPLURT...RRUUURRSPLUSH..SPLUS

"ART YOU TREASURE. ART I LOVE."

WE MUST ACT TOGETHER TO PROTECT AND PRESERVE YOUR HUSBAND'S LEGACY FOR THE AGES.

SO THE WORLD WILL NOT FORGET HIS EXISTENCE OR HIS CREATIVE HEART! LET ME HELP YOU DO THIS, NORMANDIE.

SIGN THIS PAPER, SO I CAN REPRESENT YOU--

--SPEAK FOR YOU TO THOSE ART DEALER SCAVENGERS WHEN WE GET BACK TO CIVILIZATION.

RRRRUURRRR...RRRRUURRRR...SPLURTT...RRUURRRRSH

SPLURTT...SPLUSHH... RRRRUURRRRRUURRRR...SPLUSH

WHAT'S YOUR PROBLEM, FOSTER? WHAT ARE YOU LOOKING SO DOWN IN THE MOUTH ABOUT?

NOTHING. NOT A THING. I WAS ON THE WINNING SIDE, WASN'T I?

RRRRUURRRR...SPLUUSH...SPLURTSPLURTRRUURR...

WHEN YOU'RE WITH THE J-MAN, WHAT OTHER SIDE COULD YOU BE ON?

RRRRUURRRR...SPLUUSH...SPLURTSPLURT...RUURR...

RRRRUUR RR...SPLUUSH...RRRRRRRRUURRRR...SPLURT

THE J-MAN'S NEVER BEEN WITH A PRETTY WOMAN LIKE THE WIDOW, NORMANDIE.

RRRRUURRRR...SPLUUSH...RRRRRRRRUURRRR...SPLURT

SOME MEN GET TO HAVE PRETTY WOMEN SMILE AT THEM, YOU KNOW.

AND SAY NICE THINGS TO THEM.

AND DO NICE THINGS FOR THEM.

SPLUUSH...RRRR...SPLUURT...RRRRRRRRUURRRURR

THE WIDOW NEVER GAVE THE J-MAN AS MUCH AS A SMILE.

SHE'LL TAKE NOTICE OF THE J-MAN WHEN I CLUB HER WITH YOU, HOW MUCH YOU WANT TO BET?

RRRRUURRRR...SPLUUSH...RRRRRRRUURRRR...SPLURT

SPLURT...RRRRUURRRR...SLURRRRP..RUURRRRRR..RUURP

RRRUURRRR...SPLUUSH...RRRRRRUURRRR...SPLURT...SPLUSH

RRRRUURRRR...SPLUUSH...RRRUURR...SPLURT...SPLUSH

LOCKSPUR, YOU BETTER GET YOUR BUTT IN A GALLOP! THE WIDOW'S ONTO US! AND SHE'S HEADING BACK YOUR WAY!

IT TRULY BREAKS MY HEART TO DO THIS.

RUURRRR...SPLUUSH...RRRRRRRUURRRR...SPLURT...SPLUSH

SKRASH

SMUS

RRUURRRR...SPLUUSH...RRRUUPPPP...SPLURT...SPLUSH

WELL, WHATEVER'S GOING ON, I SEE IT'S ALL OVER. NOW WE CAN GET BACK TO WHAT WE'RE GOING TO DO ABOUT ME.

ONCE, I THOUGHT WHATEVER SOLUTION I CAME UP WITH, TO FIND YOU A SAFE PLACE, WOULD BE A SIMPLE AFFAIR.

I'M OLDER AND WISER NOW. I SEE I DIDN'T KNOW AS MUCH AS I THOUGHT I DID.

YOU'LL FIGURE SOMETHING OUT. YOU ALWAYS DO. THAT'S WHY YOU'RE THE FOX. AND IT LOOKS LIKE HERE, YOU HAD A HAPPY ENDING. YOU CAN'T ASK FOR MUCH MORE THAN THAT.

BURRRP

SPLUSK

Don't miss ZORRO Graphic Novel # 4– "Flights!"

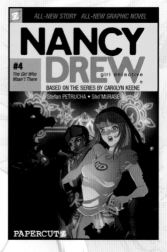